LATOYA LAWRENCE

The Session
Murder At Midnight

Contents

Foreword

Bambi is a trusted therapist who clients put their money and trust in. They share to her their innermost feelings and spill their deep darkest secrets.

Bambi thought she had heard and seen it all until this one unusual client comes in for a session and manages to get inside to pick her brain.

Bambi eventually starts to lose her grip and begins to wonder who the therapist is and who the client is.

In a head game of truth and revelation, will this new client serve as a hard nut to crack- or will Bambi end up the one to crack up enough to kill?

One

The Kill

The clock struck midnight.

Two rounds fired—one to the head, one to the chest.

The shooter slipped over the balcony and vanished into the night.

Two

Morning Routine

Tuesday, August 21st, 2012

Bambi Alexander got ready for work. All she had time for was a piece of toast and a glass of orange juice; she would have a big lunch later in the day. She grabbed her handbag and keys from the countertop, then headed out to the driveway. Inside her Lincoln MKZ, Bambi sorted papers in the glove compartment before starting the ignition.

The ride through the neighborhood onto the Grand Central Parkway was no different than usual—the same monotonous one-hour commute from suburban East Williston, Long Island, to the Upper West Side of Manhattan. Upon reaching her destination, Bambi parked on the first-level deck of the Kramden Building.

In the lobby, she greeted the door attendant, who tipped his hat. "Good morning, Mrs. Alexander," Bobby said. "I have mail for you from yesterday." The uniformed man sat across from a logbook, a telephone system, and surveillance monitors that filmed recorded interactions in the elevators and throughout the floors.

"Thank you, Bobby," Bambi said. He handed her nine items of mail bound by a thick rubber band. Bambi ascended within the silver walls of the elevator to her private office. She pulled the keys from her handbag, unlocked the door, and made herself comfortable. After removing and hanging her sable-colored suit jacket, she sifted through a pile of files on her black oakwood veneer desk. There was a new client on the schedule for later that evening: *Larina Wilder*. As a doctoral-level clinical psychologist, Bambi Alexander had a long day ahead of her.

Three

At The Department

When the lead lieutenant left for the day, Sergeant Stewart Alexander took over, supervising officers and overseeing daily operations at the Midtown North precinct on 51st Street.

The sixty-year-old bearded man, with dark hair and a fair complexion, finished his paperwork, methodically filing reports from the officers called to the home of fellow officer Chaundra Bowman. She had been shot and killed around midnight.

Aside from his administrative duties, Stewart worked directly on the streets to investigate crimes and track suspects. He took the murder of his colleague personally. This hard-nosed sergeant and his partners made it their mission to plumb the homicide and find the killer who had taken down one of their own.

Four

Client Relations

With her legs crossed, flashing her black round-toe velveteen high-heel pumps, Bambi sat with a note pad in hand thirty-minutes into her therapy session with Ray Palmer.

The chubby, clean shaven, pale complexioned thirty-year old had a foot fetish. He loved to suck toes. So much so, he drove away the women he dated with his galling compulsion.

One woman Ray had a relationship with suggested he get help when he bit and chewed off her toenail. That was the last straw, as she had not signed up to be romanticized by someone who imitated the behavior of a canine.

"I even suck my own toes?" Ray said. "I like toes. Does that make me crazy?"

Bambi smiled.

"No, although people may find the act strange or appalling, foot fascination in sexual arousal is common than you would think. For certain people, it is a part of role play where you want to be dominated. A form of submission by bowing down to the feet to kiss, lick, or to suck toes. In other cases, it is just a matter of finding feet sensual or erotic as one might any other body part depending on one's preference or fantasy. Different individuals have certain triggers. If your foot obsession interfered with other daily activities—*if you neglected your job or failed to pay your bills*—then I would say you had a problem. From what you have expressed so far does not extend anywhere other than the bedroom. You have nothing to worry about. There are crazier things that go on with people and their freaky habits. The only problem you seem to have has been maintaining relationships with women who are turned off by what became a fixation. I recommend you practice restraint on the women you deal with. Respect their boundaries and develop intimate communication so that you do not scare them off. If that does not work, try to find someone who shares a tendency for the arousal as you do. And if necessary, there are feet fetish masturbation toys for men that you can buy to tame, control, and to satisfy your desires so you can focus on a healthy relationship in other areas without overwhelming your partner."

Ray liked talking to Bambi. He appreciated how she spoke to him like a human and without judgment. She did not treat him as one beneath her to look down on or to fix.

The woman looked to find answers and solutions to enhance

or promote better well-being and without trying to impose on one's life or their personal lifestyle.

"Thank you, Mrs. Alexander. I feel a whole lot better than when I first came in. You inspire me." said the blued-eyed bundle of nerves with ash brown hair. "I am going to incorporate your counsel and apply your recommendations, and I will tell you how things work out."

Ray chuckled in his feel-good mood and relief.

The forty-nine-year-old therapist, her thick, bushy black hair falling to her shoulders, jotted down a final note before discharging her client of five months. Bambi recorded their next monthly appointment in a cranberry, leather-bound planner and handed Ray an index card—a physical reminder of their September session. As Mr. Palmer grabbed his hoodie and exited the office, Bambi rose from her chair and crossed to her desktop.

With a few clicks, she logged Ray into her billing and attendance records before pulling up the file for her final client of the day. Bambi maintained meticulous clinical logs as part of her standard procedure for assessment and counseling. She accessed this documentation to track the progress or decline of both outpatient referrals and independent visitors seeking help. As a thorough practitioner, she ensured seamless coordination of care, often collaborating with psychiatrists when clients required diagnostic observation or medication management. Her comprehensive client histories, along with insurance and billing plans, were managed by her assistant in the front office of her three-room suite.

At 5:15 p.m., Evangeline buzzed Mrs. Alexander's line to announce the arrival of a first-time client named Larina Wilder.

"Okay," Bambi said. Bent over, she was loading a stack of copy paper into the printer. "You can send her in." Bambi usually allowed intervals between visits to arrange summaries, prepare for upcoming appointments, and refresh herself mentally.

Seconds after hanging up, a tall, strikingly attractive woman with a caramel complexion walked in. Her straight, silky brown hair fell just past her shoulders. The woman moved with confidence, her solid, medium-frame body clad in knee-high brown suede boots, black skin-tight pants, and a lightweight brown cashmere turtleneck that hung below her well-rounded derriere.

Bambi heard footsteps behind her.

"Take a seat. I will be right with you." The psychologist, dressed in a cream-colored blouse and sable dress pants, kept her back turned while she finished refilling the machine. She then turned toward her desk to grasp the new file she had prepared, along with her notepad, pen, and planner.

When Bambi's dark-brown eyes finally met the stranger's, she paused. Something familiar about this unfamiliar face struck her oddly. The peculiar vibe pierced her, giving rise to a sudden caution. Bambi pushed her circumspection aside for the moment; if she felt threatened at any point, there lay a hidden button beneath her chair. In an emergency, she could press it to trigger a silent alarm on Evangeline's desk, notifying her assistant to call security.

The medium-height therapist sat down to get acquainted. Bambi exhaled, the breath wafting through the thick, satiny black strands of her trimmed bangs as she forced herself to relax.

"Hello, how are you?" Bambi said to the woman who sat with poise and who had watched her every move since she first entered the office.

"How do you do?" Larina said in a voice that sounded friendly and confident. Judging by the woman's tone and body language, Bambi thought it fair to assume that, despite the eerie first impression, the air seemed clear of any problematic episode.

Bambi politely interrupted before she could move further into the session, but Larina cut in briefly. "That perfume you are wearing smells wonderful. May I ask what fragrance that is?"

Flattered that the woman complimented her taste in scent, Bambi answered generously with a smile. "It is Enchanted Embrace by Deveraux. It just came out. I bought two bottles from Goldman's Department Store. *I love it*. It lasts all day long and does not cause irritation. It is a high-quality, top-of-the-line, brand-name perfume."

Larina, with her legs and arms crossed in sophistication, nodded her head in assent as if she was impressed. "Goldman's is an expensive store."

Moving along to avoid responding about her personal spending habits, Bambi addressed her client professionally to get on with what had brought Miss Wilder to therapy.

"I am going to tell you as I tell all my clients: *this is a free environment.* I want you to feel comfortable, not like you must walk on eggshells, worried about how I will perceive you or what I will write down and classify you as. I am not here to judge or condescend; I am here to listen and help alleviate the concerns you want to discuss. I am here to get to know you, the person—to help you become the best version of yourself and cut through anything standing in the way of your wellness."

From the sound of it, the woman seemed like a real gem to trust. She had an energy that made one want to delve right in and spill their guts. Larina, however, did not go that route. She kept herself calm, cool, and cautious. She hadn't come to heal; she had come to rattle. Larina intended to push this psychologist's buttons, to challenge Bambi's position of power and seize control for herself.

"Well, I'm glad to hear that, because I plan to hold nothing back," Larina said.

"So, tell me about yourself," Bambi said. "Are you married? Do you have any children?"

"No. Are you married? Do you have any children?" Larina countered.

Bambi made a quick notation on her pad. Larina watched the pen move. The woman had just given a grand speech about not jumping to conclusions, yet there she was, noting an assumption based on a simple defensive question.

"Yes, I am married. My husband and I have no children," Bambi answered.

"Oh, that's interesting," Larina said with a smirk.

The thirty-three-year-old reached into her purse and pulled out a Newport 100. Bambi looked up from her notepad, surveying her client out of the corner of her eye.

"Do you mind if I smoke?" Larina asked. She didn't actually care if the woman was bothered.

"No. Do as you please. Whatever makes you feel relaxed," Bambi encouraged.

Larina's thin lips curled into a subtle sneer. She inhaled a long drag, exhaled a cloud of smoke, and prepared to impart her story.

"I am an occupational therapist."

The words caught Bambi off guard, forcing her to take a mental step back from her premature assessment.

She even felt a little intimidated, as this woman also held a position in a field of therapy that catered to the healing and well-being of others. One scope of therapeutic management dealt with mental health, while the other dealt with physical health recovery and mobility. Though mental illness was no issue to minimize, Bambi saw Larina's job as of greater importance, since helping a person heal physically played a vital role in contributing to their mental wellness.

Bambi nodded at Larina, impressed, as if to cheer her on. "I quit another short-lived profession before I entered this one. I find what I do now less dangerous," Larina continued.

"Oh, really?" Bambi said. "What was it that you did before?"

Larina laughed. "That will be my secret," she added with an indirect taunt.

This is an interesting character, Bambi thought. She had come across all kinds—from the peculiar to the zany to the crazy. As Larina studied the psychologist's face and body language in a way Bambi hadn't realized, she continued.

"I grew up in Cherry-town, Brooklyn, with my father, mother, and two sisters. My mother was a careerist who cared more about her job than she did her own family. So much so, that she eventually abandoned us all."

Oh. This one has mommy issues, Bambi thought. "Did your mother's choice to pick up and leave anger you?"

"Down the line," Larina said, puffing on her cigarette. "At first, I was in shock. I mean, I knew she resented having a family, but

I did not think she would disappear on us like she did."

"How did she show resentment and regret?"

"As children, we used to vie for our mother's attention. She didn't even have a favorite—she did not take a fondness to any of us girls. As we grew older, we tried to please her by taking an interest in the things she cared about. We even made career plans to gain her approval, yet it did no good. I remember when she would get angry at my sisters and me, or my father. She always said she wished she'd never had children or a husband because she could have had the life she wanted. Once she left, we found out through our father that when she got pregnant with me, she considered me a mistake. She married my father, ended up with two other children, and then felt trapped."

Bambi made eye contact with Larina.

"That sounds cruel for a mother to say to her young children— as if it was your fault that she 'messed up' her life. I don't understand women like that. If she did not want children, she should have been more responsible. She did not have to get married and continue to have children if she didn't want to."

Larina did not respond to Bambi's words. She tapped her Newport, dumping ashes into the glass receptacle on the end table, which was decorated with a Clivia miniata bush lily.

Five

The Second Kill

Thursday, August 30th, 2012

Kennedy Daughtler lay across the disrupted bed sheets, nude and relaxed. Her soft, pale skin was still moist from perspiration and the friction of intercourse. Her charismatic lover, Doug, had just left the apartment to catch the elevator.

A fleeting character exiting the shaft went unnoticed as Doug, a tall man of dark complexion, entered the elevator in a rush, still tucking in his shirt. He glanced slyly at the closing doors to snatch a quick view of the man whose head was bowed, preoccupied with correcting his appearance.

The doorbell to apartment E16 rang. The time was 11:59 p.m. Kennedy arose from the damp sheets with a smile. Doug must have forgotten something. Maybe they could go for round two if he were up for it—he could always tell his wife of four years that he'd been stuck at work.

Still baring her essentials, the expectant woman paced from her bedroom to welcome her lover back into her arms. But as Kennedy unlocked the door to her third-floor unit, she was met with a gunshot to the head and another to the chest.

Six

Home

❧

Friday, August 31st, 2012

The last two weeks of August felt like autumn—cold and brisk. Bambi scrambled through her closet in search of the insulated black and grey hooded coat she fancied. The casual, weather-resistant apparel had kept her warm throughout many fall seasons; she'd paid top dollar for the item, yet it had apparently disappeared without a trace. Standing in only her bra, socks, and underwear, Bambi stood baffled on the carpeted floor.

Stewart entered the back door of their Long Island home puffing on a cigar. A man of meaty flesh, he had spent hours in the city following the death of a fellow police officer. A member of the force had phoned the sergeant shortly after midnight after tenants reported gunshots; Officer Kennedy Daughtler was found stretched out in her third-floor doorway by Mrs.

Jenna Taylor from apartment E18.

Blood puddled on the tiled floors. One bullet had entered Kennedy's forehead and exited the back of her head, leaving her almond-shaped blue eyes stiff and wide. Red fluid also leaked profusely from a wound between her bare breasts. Though Stewart had seen a plethora of gruesome murders throughout his career, this was a comrade he knew personally. The scene penetrated his mind.

By 6:23 am, Bambi heard footsteps on the staircase. 'Have you seen my Bauer Sinclair coat?' she asked as Stewart entered the bedroom. Knowing the designer well—as his wife owned several of his pieces—Stewart simply answered, 'No.'

'That's odd. I've looked everywhere. Are you sure you didn't move it?'

'Yes, honey. I'm sure.' Exhausted and ready to catch a snooze before his afternoon shift, Stewart removed his coffee-colored military parka and hung it up. He rested his cigar in an ashtray, stripped to his underwear, and fell fast asleep under the covers.

Seven

Work

Later that afternoon, around 3:17 p.m., a wallet found at the crime scene was identified as belonging to Douglas Finnegan. Recognized as an officer from the Midtown North Precinct on 51st Street, Douglas was questioned at the station in the office of his supervisor. Sergeant Alexander shut the door to speak with his subordinate in private.

The officer sat across a desk of scattered paperwork. His eyes shifted nervously from the tan bulletin board to the brown file cabinets, then to the closed white mini-blinds.

"Would you like a cup of coffee?" the overweight, bearded sergeant asked, adjusting his dusty-blue tie.

"Ah, no sir." The brown-eyed man felt too anxious to drink; he could barely sit still.

Alexander poured himself a cup from the coffee maker before reclining in his seat to canvass the fellow officer. "Okay. You know the drill," he said. "Officer Kennedy Daughtler was shot twice and killed this morning. We found your wallet in her apartment. Can you tell me how it got there?"

Hesitant to give a straight admission, Douglas chose to fib. "Kennedy drove me back to her place late last night after work. We had a couple of beers and I left. My wallet must have accidentally fallen out of my jacket pocket."

Alexander glared at Finnegan with piercing gray eyes. A hard-boiled, pragmatic veteran, he sniffed bullshit he wasn't in the mood for. "So," the sergeant uttered sarcastically, "then that means the semen found on her sheets and up her twat won't come back as yours once we collect a DNA sample?"

Douglas panicked, though he tried his darnedest not to show it. Then he relented.

"Alright, alright," Douglas said. He hated when the sergeant gave him "the eye." It was like a lion about to devour its prey for serving him the wrong flavor of a dish. "We were sexually involved. I was in such a rush to leave I ended up dropping my wallet. I didn't know it was missing until the cab I flagged arrived at my home and I couldn't pay him. I informed the driver that I was a police officer, wrote my name and number on the back of his business card, and promised to eventually pay him."

"Why didn't you just say that from the get-go? This is not a game of cat and mouse; this is your job. You want to play games, you can turn in your badge and head out the door. This is a serious matter. Another one of our own—shot and killed in the same manner as Officer Chaundra Bowman a week ago."

"Yes. I am aware of that, sir."

With everything out in the open, the tension dissipated, relieving a bit of the stress Douglas had felt. He was now up for that cup of hot coffee Stewart had offered at the start.

"Get up and get it yourself," the sergeant said coldly.

Stewart reached into the left pocket of his shirt for a cigar. By the time he lit the plump stem and took several deep puffs, Douglas had returned to his seat with a scalding cup of coffee blended with milk and sugar.

"About what time did you leave Kennedy's apartment?"

"Uh," Douglas said after blowing over his beverage, then sparingly sipping the steaming liquid. "At almost midnight. I remember looking at my watch. I promised my wife I would be home by ten o'clock. I was already two hours late from fooling around with Kennedy, and I didn't want to disappoint Gloria again."

"Did you see or notice anyone or anything on your way out?"

"No. Someone did get off the elevator, but I didn't get a look at them. I didn't pay any attention to the person."

"Unfortunately, there are no surveillance cameras in the building, and no one saw this individual or any other suspicious characters to get a description. It looks like we may have a police killer on our hands. One geared toward the police here at our department."

Before excusing Douglas from his presence, Stewart Alexander felt the need to ask one further question that pressed on his mind. "How long had you and Miss Kennedy been seeing one another under wraps?"

The tall, dark-complexioned man with dark hair, dark eyes, and no facial hair uttered, "For about eight months."

A sour expression dominated the sergeant's embittered face. If looks could kill, Douglas would have dropped dead on the spot.

Eight

Dinner

Five round tier crystal chandeliers hung above elegant tables dressed in deep red tablecloths there at Le Petit Chateau where Bambi and her husband dined on French cuisine with guests. Personal friends and colleagues of the therapist—Dr. Jillian and Ryan Elsher—a married couple who were both psychiatrists and occupied their private practice—delighted in an evening of wine, laughs, and an engaging get-together.

As Stewart preferred to have entertained himself anywhere other than here with Bambi and her high-class physician-psychologist ensemble, he promised not to smoke any of those foul-smelling, nasty cigars he had a fondness for and an addiction to. The veteran police officer really needed one right now. He needed something strong to help him endure through the rest of the night other than the expensive wine they all took dainty sips on.

If he had to hear about another one of their clients and who had gotten prescribed what and who recently jumped out the window of a twenty-two-story building, he thought he would explode.

"I do not want to sit here all evening and listen to this boring-me-mad shit."

At least the food tasted good. Stewart could not deny or complain about the top-rate succulent French fare.

Nine

The Third Kill

Tuesday, September 4th, 2012

At a quarter to 11 p.m., Madison Farlowe walked into the station, coming off the beat from patrolling with her partner, Gerri. The thirty-three-year-old, brown-complexioned woman with thick, shoulder-length, dark-auburn hair headed to her locker to change clothes. She locked up her duty handgun, ensuring she had a compact weapon for protection on the way home.

"Have a good night, Maddy," Detective Levine said as she strolled down the hall.

"Thank you, sir," the tall, soft-spoken, off-duty officer responded.

"See you tomorrow," chimed in another officer. "Don't forget, after work we're going to go chill over at Grady's for the anniversary bash."

"Okay," Madison uttered with a smile on her tired-looking face. Although the first thing she wanted to do was go to sleep, she knew she had to do two or three late-night chores around the house.

Inside her car, Madison strapped on her seat belt, sent a text to her fiancé, and turned the key to commute from Manhattan to her Copeland, New Jersey, home. As she drove down the damp streets through the drizzling rain, the radio played a symphony of catchy tunes. She listened to the disc jockey, the commercial breaks, and the brief news reports until she pulled into her driveway.

Madison exited her dark-blue Ford Fiesta at 11:57 p.m. She grabbed the handles of the two empty trash cans, which had been knocked over by the wind, and rolled them back toward the locked garage doors. The rain had intensified in New Jersey. After securing the large receptacles inside the dry, sheltering garage, she re-locked the doors and headed for her house. The chilly, windy precipitation was becoming hard to bear.

Just as Madison appeared at the end of the driveway, walking around to the front of her attached brick home, an individual emerged from the shadows of the rainy night to surprise the unsuspecting officer with a brutal gunshot to the head and another to her chest.

Ten

The Last Straw

Wednesday, September 5th, 2012

Tears fell heavily from Sally Ventura's light-brown eyes as she recounted the traumatic events that haunted her from childhood. Secrets buried long ago were triggered by a recent incident, resurfacing to disturb what once didn't bother Sally a bit, as memory had faded.

Bambi sat in her counseling session, snug in the beige, mid-century accent lounge armchair, comforted by a back pillow. Thirty-one-year-old Sally lay upon the marzipan-colored, traditional-style, plush-textured, upholstered couch that occupied the office where the psychologist's framed credentials and art portraits hung on the buckwheat-colored walls.

Bambi wrote down notes before recommending a choice of

well-qualified psychiatrists she suggested Sally visit. The woman, whose schedule ran busy that day, handed the unsettled client four referrals who took her insurance and welcomed Sally to future sessions if she chose not to accept the offer of further psychiatric help to delve deeper into her complicated personal issues.

In the meantime, Bambi checked emails and caught up on calls between other clients. Afterwards, the psychotherapist conducted a teletherapy session. During the hour-long video conference over the internet, Bambi encouraged, advised, and praised a gentleman named Van Hawke, who had made vast improvements in his lifestyle since she had last spoken to him.

A half hour later, Larina Wilder walked into Bambi Alexander's private office. Evangeline, immersed in billing and other clientele paperwork, sent the woman in for her five p.m. session.

Two weeks had passed since Larina's first visit. Here she presented herself a second time to challenge, vent, and release emotion.

The first thing Larina noticed is that Bambi did not have on any lipstick as she remembered.

"Yeah," Bambi muttered, partially distracted. "I could not find my color. I misplaced the tube somewhere and I did not have time to look for it."

The professional held documents in hand that she went to do a quick scope through prior to engaging in their meeting.

"You must have really liked that shade to not substitute another instead," Larina said as she relaxed herself in one of the tufted, upholstered visitor chairs selected and situated to ease clients.

"When is the last time you had sex Mrs. Alexander?"

Bambi raised her head from the papers she held. The thick straight bushy black locks of her hair swayed gently in unison to her movements.

"—Excuse me," she said, her eyes widening slightly. The woman mildly ticked, grimaced, yet she kept professional. "My personal life is not up for discussion."

The tall, brown-eyed lady with a caramel shade of light-brown skin had gotten a rise out of the psychologist she aspired to tease and torment.

"Well, I would like to talk about my sex life," Larina put forth bluntly.

"The last time I was here," she continued, while she crossed her legs. "I discussed my mother. Now I will discuss what is tying her to me. I am like my mother in a certain way. When she left us— not only did she leave to lead her own life— she left us to spend that life with another man she preferred over my father."

Bambi sat still in her chair. She listened intently, and absorbed Larina's revelatory words.

"I involved myself with a married man. We met in the workplace. He is not one that I would usually go for, but it gave me a thrill to know I excited and appealed to him in ways that his wife could not— though I did not really want him."

"You saw this sexual relationship as an approach to feed your ego?" Bambi asked, firmly.

"Absolutely not," Larina said. "I do not suffer from self-confidence or self-esteem issues."

"Well, if you did not want this man and it flattered you that you stimulated or enraptured him in ways that his wife did not, and as you claim there was no need to fill a void, what is your gain? Do you or did you enjoy the sex? Do you like his company or conversation?"

Larina's thin-shaped lips turned into a fleeting smirk.

"It is not about the sex. I am not hard up for sex or for anyone's company or conversation. Him sticking it to me was sticking it to his wife. You see, he gave her my bladder infection."

Revolted by her client's distasteful comment, Bambi cut in.

"—Oh, come on now. That was asinine, uncalled for."

An outlandish chortle roared out from Larina, adding to her rudeness. This woman was obnoxious indeed. Though it was an arduous task to deal with her—fitful and erratic in all sorts of ways—it came with the territory.

"Did you personally know the wife of your coworker to intentionally do such a thing? Is that all you gave them, or did you give them anything more? Infections are nothing to take lightly, and as a person in your field of work, I am surprised. You are an occupational therapist. Do you like hurting people?"

"Speaking of occupational—it was a different occupation. Oh, and do not act like such a goody-two-shoes with me, hon. I am sure you have a skeleton or two packed away deep inside your closet."

"What are you talking about?" Bambi asked, ignoring Larina's latter remarks. "What different occupation?"

"The dangerous one I mentioned to you last time I was here." A stony-hearted expression dominated Larina's face. Her brown eyes were direct, bold, and intense. She sat upright, relaxed, and confident. In the narrow space between them, Bambi stared blankly at Larina, guarded.

"I am sorry. I do not recall. You will have to remind me," the psychotherapist said.

"To answer your first question, no. I guess you can say that I did not personally know the wife. I just know what he told me about her. He was not only a coworker that I regularly slept with; he was my boss. I used to work as a police officer. He had an eye for us young gals. Ever since his wife had a hysterectomy, she no longer satisfied him. He said he couldn't feel her organs and that horrible scar from the surgery—"

Bambi had heard enough of this crude and insolent hussy. She no longer had the patience for her. She wanted Larina out of the office at once.

"Alright, enough. This is not going to work out. I think you would do better to find another therapist to consult with. I am not the one for you."

Both women rose to their feet. Larina collected her hat, jacket, and scarf from a nearby chair, then uttered one last remark.

"I guess as a psychologist, you are not all you're supposed to be. If you quit in the middle of a session because you can't manage it, what good are you?"

"Get out." Bambi stepped over to her desk to buzz Evangeline's line. "Cancel all future appointments scheduled for Larina Wilder and close her account—I will no longer service her as a client. Do not accept any requests from Miss Wilder. As of now, ban her from this office."

The receptionist acted quickly upon her supervisor's words. Evangeline's fingers went to work, typing at the keyboard. The petite brunette wondered what had taken place in the back room to rile Bambi to such an extent. If only Evangeline could have been a fly on the wall to capture the rift that had just occurred.

Eleven

Uneasy

Instrumental music from the living room CD player drifted into the dining room, where Bambi Alexander sat alone, barely touching her dinner.

A glass of chardonnay sat beside a plate of roast beef and mashed potatoes that had grown cold. Her appetite was lost in preoccupied thoughts as she picked at her food.

Usually the one to lend an ear and help resolve the issues of others, Bambi now struggled to solve the conflict rising within herself.

Later that evening, perched in bed against two firm pillows with her reading glasses on, she leafed through a book she had no interest in. She was just killing time, waiting for her husband to arrive home—whenever that might be.

Twelve

Under Critical Examination

The Midtown North Precinct had a cop-killer on their hands—
one who specifically targeted the department on 51st Street.

On Tuesday, inside her second-floor New York City condo-
minium, thirty-eight-year-old Chaundra Bowman, a fifteen-
year veteran of the force, was shot and killed as she slept. On
Friday, August 31st, thirty-five-year-old Kennedy Daughtler
was shot and killed in the doorway of her Lower East Side
apartment. And today, Wednesday, September 5th, thirty-three-
year-old Madison Farlowe was shot and killed in the driveway
of her Copeland, New Jersey home.

All murders occurred at or around midnight, with each victim
shot twice: once in the head and once in the chest.

While there were still no leads on a physical description, the

"

unknown killer had begun to leave behind a small trail of evidence currently under the microscope.

It was odd that the killer had suddenly become sloppy. *Was it a slip?* Police realized it was either a ploy to throw law enforcement off, a game crafted to goad and challenge them, or the killer wasn't so bright after all—simply lucky the first two times.

Thirteen

Off Duty

Stewart Alexander made it from the city to East Williston, Long Island, at a quarter to midnight. He pulled up in front of his five-bedroom, five-bathroom, two-car garage, stunningly impressive two-story house.

The man, sapped of energy, stepped from the Nissan Altima he drove. Weathering the unfriendly climate until he reached the frosted mahogany-glass doors, Stewart entered the pathway that led through the gourmet kitchen. The spectacular abode, which gave off an abundance of light and boasted style and space, greeted him with a warm reception. There was no place like home.

Stewart intended to hit the shower before retiring for the night. Overtaxed and overloaded by his duties and the ensuing new protocols following recent homicide events against workmates on the force, the aging man longed for breathing space. With the opportunity to pause, relax, and decide what to do next away from other people, the long-time sergeant could re-evaluate and conduct an updated approach during this overriding period.

At the bedroom doorway, Stewart saw Bambi positioned upright on the cotton-sheeted mattress. She sat against the headboard beside the dimmable lamp of the ornamented nightstand. In the welcoming, soft-lit ambiance that faintly glowed from where he stood, the thick-set man, still dressed in his coat, tread across the Saxony-textured carpet.

The moment her husband walked into the room, Bambi removed her reading glasses and placed her closed book onto the decorated nightstand. The forty-nine-year-old, mildly distressed woman folded her knees into her chest, wrapping both arms around her legs with beady eyes that followed Stewart's every move. From the discard of his chewing gum to the removal of his hat, the hanging of his coat, and the sliding off of his shoes, Bambi watched attentively.

When he returned from the adjoining bathroom, Bambi broke her silence. Water beaded from the shower, running in firm streams to reach a suitable temperature. Stewart sat and leaned his body weight on his side of the bed while he lazily undressed.

"Do you know a Larina Wilder?" Bambi asked.

"Who?" Steward said.

"Larina Wilder."

"No. Who is she?" Steward asked, removing his socks.

"A client I had in my office. A very rude and disrespectful woman who says she used to work as a cop."

"And?" Steward said. He wondered why Bambi brought up the woman and where she was going with this.

"This woman came to see me twice—two weeks ago, and again today. At both sessions, she appeared to indirectly throw attacks at me. Today, I had to throw her out of my office. She had gotten too vulgar and personal, as if she were insinuating things that pertained to me—*and maybe even you.*"

Steward rolled his hooded grey eyes and sighed through chapped lips that had cracked in the recent blast of cool September weather. "You know that many of those patients of yours are nuts. Why are you letting it get to you? Pay the woman no mind." He reached over and pecked Bambi on the cheek before heading to the bathroom. "Ignore whatever she said. She is just messing with your head. I deal with that kind of bullshit every day."

As a professional, Mrs. Alexander did not feel assuaged. The man's words had not put her at ease. What went on with Larina earlier in the day was hard for her to dismiss. Claims that had rung from Larina's mouth were too coincidental, relatable in negative ways by their similarities. Uncomfortably reminded by the likeness of her own unpleasant experiences, Bambi could not shrug off the vexing sensation that inexplicably hounded her.

Fourteen

The Fourth Kill

Friday, September 14, 2012

Blonde and blue-eyed, Betty Jenkins rode the elevator down from her fifth-floor apartment on the Upper West Side. It was a routine they both knew: *every night after work, she walked Barney.*

The German Shepherd—a sable powerhouse of tan and black—pulled vigorously ahead, dragging her past high-rises and luxury storefronts. Betty struggled to keep pace as the wind whipped her golden-amber curls into a frizzy tangle. Barney panted heavily, his tail wagging at full tilt and his dark eyes alert.

As they moved toward the upscale outskirts of the neigh-borhood, the sidewalks emptied. The biting night air drove the last of the pedestrians indoors, leaving the streetlamps to illuminate nothing but pavement. Betty huddled into her hooded black puffer coat, one hand gripping the leash while the other clutched her arm for warmth.

As Barney hauled her around the corner of West 31st Street, they collided with a stranger. The pavement was desolate. Suddenly, a gun appeared.

Betty took a blow to the head, then another to the chest. Her olive-complexioned face snapped back before her athletic frame slumped harshly against the ground. Barney barked uncontrollably at the thunder of gunfire.

As his owner's body gave its final, rhythmic jerks of life, the dog lunged. He tore at the stranger—a figure hidden behind black gloves, a dark hat, and a heavy scarf.

A third shot rang out. The Shepherd collapsed instantly.

The shooter vanished into the arctic silence of the empty street. The time was 12:01 a.m. Another female officer lay dead, the latest victim of an unrelenting cop-killer.

Fifteen

Le Petit Chateau

Friday, October 5th, 2012

Three weeks had passed. Bambi spent her lunch break at the French restaurant she occasionally frequented. She was greeted by a well-mannered host who seated the psychologist at an exquisite window-side booth in the VIP section. Bambi removed her coat, hat, scarf, and gloves, making herself comfortable at the elegantly set table.

While her face was buried in a menu featuring an undecidable array of enticing cuisine, the unsuspecting woman felt a shadow hover eerily over her. Standing there, dressed in a trendy, camel-colored wool wrap coat with belted shoulder panels, was a familiar face. Bambi raised her head, her disappointment immediate.

"What are you doing here?" Bambi asked.

The woman's tone was arrogant. "I could ask you the same thing. Is this not a public place?"

Bambi tossed the menu onto the red tablecloth, which featured scalloped edges and a delicate lace floral design. "What? Are you following me now?" the therapist asked, livid.

The tall woman—solid of frame with silky, light-brown skin—gracefully untied her belt and took a seat across from the irate, flushed-faced Bambi. *The nerve of this she-devil.* Larina Wilder, the off-putting client Bambi had ousted from her office a month ago, had the audacity to intrude on her former therapist's lunch.

Bambi glared as the insolent young woman removed her vintage, French-style wool fedora. Her center-parted brown hair, which usually hung sleekly past her shoulders, was clipped neatly into a barrette. Dazzling, water-drop-shaped opal gems hung from Larina's ears, and a flower-shaped, eighteen-karat gold-plated pearl necklace sparkled against her smooth skin. An eighteen-karat gold zircon bracelet adorned Larina's left wrist, while a matching flower-shaped bangle wrapped around her right.

Bambi could not deny that Larina was an attractive woman with impeccable style. Her outward appearance was perfectly assembled, yet the person inside required an extensive reconstruction. Larina clutched the menu Bambi had cast onto the table. "Well, what will we have for lunch?"

The baffled psychologist, accustomed to dealing with diverse pathologies in her line of work, could not understand the woman's fixation on pestering her. Bambi gathered her things to request another table, but as she moved, haunting, spiteful words escaped Larina's thin, upturned lips.

"How long has it been since you left the force? It seems we have a great deal in common. We were both police officers. We both slept with our department supervisors. In fact, we slept with the same supervisor. You and I both enjoyed a great deal of 'preferential' supervision."

Bambi paused. Perturbed and curious, she dropped her handbag, coat, and scarf back onto the chair. She resumed her seat by the window to stare directly into Larina's stony brown eyes.

"How do you know I used to be a cop?" Bambi asked in a low, hushed, yet firm tone. Under the surface, she seethed. Ordinarily, she would have walked away without a second thought, yet Larina held a subtle control over her. The woman had the power to affect her emotions and confound her brain.

Bambi struggled against the manipulation; she was a psychotherapist, for heaven's sake. How could she allow a patient to "doctor" and distort her this way? At forty-nine, she had to face the truth: *Larina had hit too close to home.* There was something familiar about this stranger who spewed secrets from Bambi's own life—things no one should have known.

"Is your husband not a police officer? Didn't you meet him on the force?"

"Yes," Bambi said. "How do you know that?"

"I know a lot of things about you," Larina replied.

Bambi sat there, frustrated and discomfited. She believed Larina held information worthy of her attention—details she didn't want to hear but needed to confront for her own advantage.

"Tell me then," Bambi said.

Bambi, wearing a fashionable white knitted turtleneck with luxuriant black hair that hung voluminously over her shoulders, seemed to gain a new sense of backbone. Bambi's aim was to let Larina talk—to let her run her big mouth until she found a way to use reverse psychology to turn the tables, giving the woman a taste of her own medicine.

"I asked my husband if he knew you," Bambi added. "He told me he didn't."

"*Wow*. How quickly you catch on," Larina sneered. "Our counsel wasn't unfruitful after all. I made you think. I'm inside your head, and it only took two sessions. You were always strong in building your career, I'll give you that—but you're weak everywhere else."

"Who are you?" Bambi asked.

"I am one of Stewart's ex-lovers. He must have forgotten. With all the women he hopped into bed with at the department, he probably lost track." Larina dropped the menu onto the table with a sharp thwack.

The thirty-three-year-old menace grabbed her hat and coat, ready to leave. "Revenge is a dish best served cold. There is nothing on this menu appetizing enough for me."

That was it? Bambi thought. She watched Larina walk away with an arrogant, confident gait. A sweet, fruity floral scent of vanilla, berry, mint, and lilac lingered in the air. The fragrance was familiar—Enchanted Embrace by Deveraux, the same one she had bought years ago at Goldman's.

Bambi reached into her purse for her smartphone and sent an urgent text to her confidante, Jillian Elsher, the psychiatrist she had dined with five weeks earlier.

Sixteen

The Homicide Division— Tracking Down A Murderer

Stewart Alexander worked overtime at the department under the supervision of Lieutenant Mel Fuller.

During the past three weeks, the department had lost another three female employees to the brutal slaying of a homicidal killer whom police were closing in on. Officer Darlene Keller was murdered on Tuesday, September 18th; Officer Jane Ford was killed on Monday, September 24th; and Susan Thatcher was shot yesterday, Thursday, October 4th.

The investigation continued to turn up a revealing line of evidence and a strong lead to apprehend the suspect.

As law enforcement hoped to solve the 'Midtown Unit Murder Case' and conduct an official arrest, circumstances boiled over in preparation for a showdown to avenge their fallen fellow officers. This cop-killer was the top priority at the 51st Precinct.

Strict orders had been issued to capture the individual by any means necessary—dead or alive—a decision held firmly as both necessary and legally acceptable.

Seventeen

In A Session Of Her Own

Bambi canceled and postponed her afternoon appointments. She had her assistant and receptionist, Evangeline, manage all correspondence and future reschedules.

The jumbled, nervous psychotherapist ended up on the couch of her psychiatrist and affiliate partner. Seeking advice and a respected opinion in addition to emotional support, Bambi treated it as more of a personal consultation than a clinical one.

She met with Dr. Jillian, who headed her own private office apart from her husband, Ryan, who also practiced psychiatry.

Eighteen

A Peace Of Mind

Jillian had prescribed a mild sedative to help calm Bambi's nerves and ease her insomnia. The worked-up psychotherapist felt relieved after the discussion she shared with a woman in her same field. Bambi stopped at the pharmacy, then drove an hour from the Upper West Side of Manhattan to the village of East Williston in North Hempstead.

She knew not to expect Stewart home anytime soon; his demanding schedule and on-call shifts were inherently unpredictable. Lately, with the rise in police killings—which Stewart rarely spoke about to avoid jeopardizing investigations—Bambi hardly saw her husband at all.

Bambi stood in her pajamas on the balcony, leaning against the contemporary, translucent fencing of the glass balustrade. From the second-floor facade, the crisp evening air brought a sense of stillness. Moonlight penetrated the darkness, creating a soft, wonderful ambiance. When it grew too chilly to remain on the balcony, she shut the panoramic doors and slipped under the covers.

As she reached to turn off the stained-glass lamp on her nightstand, a notification chimed. Bambi snatched the phone. It was an anonymous text from an unrecognized number with photos attached. The message was enough to shatter the peace she had found with Jillian that afternoon. Despite the sedative, Bambi knew this would keep her awake for the rest of the night.

Nineteen

Riddle

Following her instructions, Bambi dressed and headed for the tedious drive from her home on Long Island back to the private office in Manhattan. She fought the creeping tiredness; drowsy behind the wheel, she hoped she wouldn't have an accident. The worn-out, off-duty therapist arrived at the Kramden building around 10:45 PM.

With sleepy eyes and windblown hair, bundled in winter garments, Bambi exited her car. From the street corner, she crossed over to meet Larina Wilder, whom she had spotted in the distance. They entered the premises in silence, greeted by Jim, the overnight door attendant.

The women remained quiet as they rode the elevator to the third floor. Larina followed Bambi into the office where Bambi typically performed psychosocial assessments, developed treatment plans, and supplied emotional guidance to her clients. Bambi flipped the light switch and locked the door behind them.

The forty-nine-year-old woman, who had reached her limit with Larina, stopped in the waiting area near the reception desk where Evangeline worked during office hours. Bambi stood there in the sweater, jacket, and scarf she had thrown over her pajamas in her haste to leave the house.

"Okay, Larina," Bambi said, fed up with the nonstop harassment. "What is the meaning of this?"

She held up her smartphone. Reflected on the touchscreen were photos Larina had sent earlier that night: *pictures of Bambi's husband caught in graphic sexual acts with several police officers he worked with—Chaundra Bowman, Kennedy Daughtler, Madison Farlowe, Betty Jenkins, Darlene Keller, Jane Ford, and Susan Thatcher.*

"Your corrupt husband," Larina said, her brown eyes filled with hatred and scorn. "I know what he did."

Tall, agile, and aggressive, the thirty-three-year-old looked ready to attack, yet she held herself back.

"I remembered you. You changed your name and started over with the career and the man you left us for, but I never forgot who you were; I kept track of you for eleven years. I am your past—the past you threw away, only for it to catch up to you again.

You had the nerve to sit there and tell me you didn't understand women like my mother, who blame the children they birthed for ruining their lives. You said it was no fault of the child's, but the parent's choice or irresponsibility. Your exact words were: 'I don't understand women like that. If she didn't want children, she should have been more responsible. She didn't have to get married and continue to have children if she didn't want to.'

My name is Rae Berenger. Does that ring a bell? Oh, mother dear, what a phony hypocrite you are. Our father and the rest of us paid for your sins; now, you will pay for mine."

The photos sent in the text—which Larina had somehow obtained firsthand—were what had dragged Bambi out of bed and into the city. Despite her hesitancy to endure legal consequences if she killed in cold blood, she pondered the thought deeply. Bambi had initially decided not to let Larina leave the office alive, but she reconsidered. She could not murder her own daughter.

Struck by a jolt of enlightenment, Bambi stood in thought, bereft of speech. An awkwardness dominated the room as the truth finally emerged. Everything made sense: *why Larina had entered and disrupted her life*. Bambi could no longer evade the truth. She had abandoned the children she heartlessly disowned. The deeds of a selfish woman had fostered a repercussion that inevitably rebounded to reveal its ugly head.

Within the four walls of the professional, functionally designed office, Larina and Bambi locked eyes. They spoke to one another through conscious and unconscious gestures. Already wrapped in a blanket of guilt, Bambi did not know how to respond—even with all her training and experience in psychology. This was a case where no traditional research or study applied.

In this soul-searching moment, Larina walked away from her estranged mother for the last time. She walked out of Bambi's life, never to return.

Twenty

The Shocker

Saturday, October 6th, 2012

The clock read 2:14 a.m. when Bambi sauntered through the frosted mahogany glass doors of her gorgeous Long Island home, exhausted. In the butler's pantry within the gourmet kitchen, she fumbled in a cupboard for a tea bag. She filled the metallic red kettle with fresh water and placed it over a lit flame.

After warming herself by the stove for a few seconds, she heated leftovers from the fridge, moving toward the silver-and-black double-wall oven that featured an integrated luxury design.

Elegant pendant lights hung from the ceiling over a light-beige marble island, which matched the marble panels of the glossy walls. Opposite the island, a sophisticated row of toffee-colored shaker cabinets lined the open space. Bambi passed them on her way to the staircase.

She knew her husband was home; she'd seen Stewart's Nissan Altima parked at the curb when she pulled into the driveway. The sixty-year-old bearded sergeant, who stood five feet nine inches tall, remained poised beside the bed in full uniform when his spouse entered the room. Bambi walked over to Stewart, who held a plump brown cigar that wafted thick, irritating smoke.

"What is this?" Bambi asked, shoving the screen of her Android directly into his view.

Stewart's expression was dour—one of pure sternness. He took the phone from Bambi's shivering hand. He glanced at the images with his grey eyes and asked critically, "Is this why you did it?"

"What?" Bambi said, already enveloped in a fit of rage and disappointment.

"Is this the reason you killed them?" Stewart repeated, firm in his stance. He clarified his accusation as he questioned her. Bambi, unaware of what he implied, grew further annoyed; his words incited only confusion.

"Killed them? Killed who? Stewart, what are you talking about? You are fucking women on your job—"

"Stop it, Bambi. Just stop it," Stewart demanded. The fair-complexioned man held his cigar between the joints of his sweaty, chubby fingers, his voice heavy with disdain.

This gesture of contempt made Bambi pause. *What exactly is taking place here? Why is he acting this way?* Though clueless to his assertion, she knew enough to realize something was dangerously wrong. Yet he would not listen, nor let her get a word in. Whenever she tried to question him, he acted already convinced of a guilt she knew nothing about. The police officer she had married had suddenly begun to treat her like a common criminal.

"We at the department have a stack of evidence that leads back to you for the murders of seven police officers—including the eighth death that took place two hours ago."

Bambi stood frozen beside the bed, still wrapped in her sweater, jacket, and scarf. The aroma of the food she had heated in the oven rose from the kitchen downstairs; the tea kettle began its high-pitched whistle. The sudden tension between them had pushed the mundane world aside.

"Are you insane? You cannot honestly stand there and suggest that I am responsible for murdering police officers. What has gotten into you? How could you even say that to me?"

Stewart looked at the tawny-complexioned woman, her thick, voluminous hair disheveled from the wind outside. "Where were you this morning?" he asked sharply. "Where did you just come in from? It is after 2 a.m. Officer Bertha Caddel was found killed by her five-year-old son around midnight. A pair of your black rabbit-fur gloves showed up at the scene, along with your old handgun—a match for your fingerprints. On Thursday, a sheer black shawl belonging to you was found at another crime scene. We have a sum of articles left behind, including a stick of your lipstick used to write on six of the victims' mirrors. The message read Dead Mistress. Bambi, all these dead police officers are these women here on your phone."

About to panic, Bambi ran to the walk-in closet to check a drawer in the wardrobe where she kept her service weapon. The drawer was empty. The gun was gone.

"No, no, no," Bambi repeated frantically. Then it hit her. "Oh my god, she set me up. All this time, she has been setting me up. She did this. She has been in this house!"

Bambi rushed from the closet and hammered her fists against Stewart's chest. "You had her in the house—you fucked her in my house!"

Stewart grabbed her wrists and cuffed her.

"I did not do this!" she hollered. "You know I didn't! How could I have? It was Larina Wilder—my daughter. The woman you slept with. She told me herself. She's the one who sent those images to me!"

"Babe, I don't know any Larina Wilder," Stewart said, shifting into his role as sergeant as he hauled her toward the police station.

In the middle of reading her Miranda rights, Bambi called Larina by the birth name she had given her thirty-three years ago. "Rae Berenger."

The tall man paused for a moment, hit by his conscience. He did remember a Rae Berenger who once worked at the Midtown North precinct on 51st Street, a woman he'd had a short-lived affair with. He had never known her as Larina Wilder, but he now assumed Bambi had discovered the tryst and plotted to get even by killing every woman on the job he'd entertained behind her back.

Bambi faced the man she'd married sixteen years ago. They had met on the force while she was still married to her first husband, Wilder Berenger. She gazed into Stewart's aggressive eyes for one last plea.

"Please, just listen to me. But first, I need the truth: *Did you ever have Rae Berenger here? In our house? In our bed?*"

The dark-haired, bearded man, cigar balanced in the grip of his teeth, answered Bambi with a nod. He plainly uttered, "Yes."

"Then why don't you see that she did this?"

Stewart rolled his eyes and sighed. "Bambi, I have not seen Rae in years. She left the department a long time ago. What would she have to gain?"

Wrinkling her straight-groomed brows and pert button nose, Bambi fought back tears. "She is my daughter, Stewart," she said, her voice cracking. "She has hostility toward me for abandoning her, her sisters, and her father when I was young. And in a way, I am to blame. I never looked back or cared to acknowledge that I have children out there who have become adults."

She took a shaky breath, looking for any sign of empathy. "I figured they would eventually forget about me. I did not want a family; I did not want to become tied down. You see, all of this was to get back at me. I did not know who she was when she came to my office for therapy. Now I know it was all just a part of a scheme to ruin me. I did not kill anyone; you must know that. I do not understand why you are acting this way."

"Bambi, look." Stewart stepped closer. "You have experience in law enforcement. You have motive. Your gun, found at the scene, is the weapon used in all the killings—and only your fingerprints are on it. We have confiscated items of yours tying you to the crimes. We have a solid case against you."

Tears fell from Bambi's dejected brown eyes. Bound by the cold restraint of the handcuffs, she stiffened. "Rae was an officer of the law too. I am sure she is adept in conducting a professional frame-up. Will you not even investigate it? I thought you were a smart, hardcore, not-fooled-by-bullshit sergeant. Or maybe you are in this together with my daughter—is that it?"

Stewart, done wasting time, swung Bambi around and motioned her toward the door. "Do not be ridiculous," he said. The strange distrust in her husband's eyes and his inscrutable resolve caught Bambi off guard, leaving her feeling entirely defenseless.

Twenty-One

A Settled Score

Monday, November 19th, 2012

A month and two weeks had passed. Rae Berenger strolled through the automatic glass doors of Hands with Care Nursing Home and Rehabilitation Center.

The tall, caramel-complexioned woman with straight, lustrous, brown hair that hung in a flowing ponytail entered unit 202 on the second floor after signing in at the reception desk of the facility.

Confined to a medical bed and hooked to a ventilator lay Wilder Berenger, Rae Berenger's father. The fifty-year-old man had remained comatose for sixteen years after a gunshot wound to the head. Doctors had successfully removed the bullet that penetrated his skull, yet Wilder never regained consciousness.

Ruth, Wilder's sister, refused to pull the plug on her brother as she one day hoped and prayed for a miracle. Ruth had never stopped believing that Stewart Alexander had something to do with hiring the hitman who had brutally shot her brother.

Shortly after Bambi left Wilder eighteen years ago when Rae was fourteen, Sierra eleven, and Troy eight, he had set up a large trust fund for each of the girls in their names. In this trust for minors, the distribution of any monies, properties, or assets would become at once available to the children under the supervision of a legal guardian until they reached the age of eighteen, then they could manage the money themselves if their father became deceased.

Stewart, a crooked police officer back then, who down the road supposedly showed promise in becoming an upstanding officer of the law, had gotten wind of the triple sum set up for Bambi's daughters—probably through word of mouth as one never knew who knew who.

Ruth had a stubborn notion that Stewart set out to kill Wilder and have Bambi come back for the children in the two years after she had left them and recently married him at the time. Ruth wholeheartedly did not think Bambi had any part in the scheme or any knowledge of Stewart's odious plot. Bambi would never have gone along with such an act, and besides, her ignorance would have served as a benefit in the realistic portrayal of an ex-wife completely shocked by the random in-home murder of her former husband.

The treacherous plan fell through when eleven-year-old Sierra awoke to overhear violent struggling from someone who had broken into the family home the Berenger clan shared. The young lass saw her father shot and heard the culprit make a call to someone he called Alexander to inform him he completed the job.

She also overheard the perpetrator tell the person over the line that if he did not pay him on time that he would turn him in and have him stripped of his badge to do life in prison.

The man had threatened his conspirator with a voice recording of the two orchestrating the event days ahead. Sierra had revealed what she heard to her aunt Ruth who went to a local law enforcement agency who dismissed her claims after a while and did not take her seriously. Ruth assumed word through the department had gotten back to Stewart and he used his power of persuasion to overthrow an investigation in any way connected to him.

A year later, when Sierra turned twelve, she endured an attack alone at home by a stranger she stabbed and killed after he broke into the house. The man had worn a police uniform. Ruth suspected Stewart behind the incident because of what she had heard and saw fourteen months back. He had to get her out of the way in case she started to talk and become an eyewitness if Ruth sought legal help to bring Wilder's attempted murder to justice.

When Sierra went in front of a judge for killing a twenty-seven-year-old man in self-defense the judge sentenced her to a detention facility until the age of twenty-one where she was beaten, raped, and warned from planted correction officers to keep her mouth shut in the future or else she would end up dead. It turned out that a legitimate newcomer police officer broke into the home. According to the judge, there was no way to prove the young man in uniform really broke into the house. It was Sierra's word against a dead man.

Outraged at the unfair sentencing of her niece, Ruth raised a fit. Court officers had to remove her from the courtroom. She undoubtedly knew this sent police officer imprinted the handwork of Stewart Alexander. If the man had employed an unscrupulous civilian Sierra would not have gotten an eight-year juvenile incarceration. Ruth had to admit that Stewart was a dirty bastard.

Rae saw things differently than Ruth. She believed Bambi was in on the plot to kill her father and to get custody of her and her sisters until the money eventually ran out. Rae never thought her mother was innocent or clueless to what went on.

By Wilder's bedside sat twenty-seven-year-old Troy and thirty-year-old Sierra Berenger. Troy, a short, chocolate complexioned young lady with brown eyes, bushy wavy black hair that hung past her shoulders, and thick lips greeted Rae as she came through the door.

Sierra, a medium height woman who had chestnut-brown skin, dark-brown eyes, dark-brown, bushy-straight, shoulder-length hair, full lips, and a thick body frame smiled then stood to her feet to embrace Rae when she approached toward their father.

The women had not seen their older sister in three months. Rae had Sierra and Troy believe she had taken a leave to North Carolina on business when she had really gone to New York.

Ruth had Wilder transferred from a Brooklyn medical facility and moved the Berenger sisters to Delaware with her after Sierra had experienced the attack and sentencing in the year 1994. The sixty-three-year-old woman did not think it safe for them to stay in New York. During that eight to nine-year incarceration period for Sierra Ruth made trips back and forth to New York to visit her until her release in 2003.

After she hugged her sister, Rae walked over to kiss her father's forehead and grasp his lifeless and colorless hand. Rae pondered deeply as she stared at a body that grimly pumped with air. Outwardly, she had found a way to return an overdue debt. Inwardly, she felt that she had brought to Wilder the justice he profoundly deserved. Beyond the scope of feeling no remorse for what had taken place with Bambi, Rae knew on the other side of the realm she would one day have to pay her price. A cost she had accepted.

Twenty-Two

Cell Block

In a dull grey prison uniform, Bambi sat slouched upon a jail bed behind bars at Boulder Pines Correctional in Inglenook County, New York.

In the abbreviated time spent in lockup, the woman, now going on fifty, no longer recognized herself in the mirror. Bambi's once pretty, smooth-textured, light-brown skin had turned sallow, her cheeks gaunt, her hair lank, and her body undernourished. She had faded into a darkness—a place of unbearable despair.

Once a police officer, then a psychologist, she was now an inmate. Bambi did not have anyone to stand in her corner, not even the woman she had once considered a dear friend, Dr. Jillian Elsher.

Incarcerated for crimes she did not commit, everyone who used to admire and respect her had turned against her. The people who were once in her circle paid no attention to her outcries of innocence. Bambi felt extremely hurt, unloved, alone, and completely helpless—nobody believed in her.

Twenty-Three

Final Rest

Blood spatter and droplets soiled the walls and carpet near the tall, wide picture-frame window that highlighted a gorgeous view to the yard of the spectacular home Bambi once shared with her husband.

In the living room bent over on his side next to the lush, velvety, silhouette-curved, chiffon-colored sofa and two matching silhouette-curved accent chairs lay Sergeant Stewart Alexander.

The corpulent flesh of his body had turned pale and reeked. Stiffness had developed in his joints and muscles from the onset of rigor mortis. A gunshot wound to the head and another to the chest had sealed the sixty-year-old man's fate.

About the Author

LaToya Lawrence grew up in Queens, New York. Aside from writing LaToya loves puppies, crocheting, healthy living, and nurturing her inborn spirituality.

Also by LaToya Lawrence

A Date With Murder: The Session Part II: Visiting Hours

Ex-police officer turned psychologist Bambi Alexander has been stripped of her license and sentenced to life in prison for the execution-style murders of eight female officers from her husband's precinct in Midtown Manhattan. Bambi swears she was framed, yet her cries of innocence fall on deaf ears.

But when her husband, Sergeant Stewart Alexander—who had numerous sexual encounters with the victims—is found dead in the home they once shared, the mystery deepens. While Bambi remains locked behind bars, a new string of unrelated murders begins to heat up the city streets. Was the wrong person convicted, or does Bambi have an accomplice finishing what she started?

Poise: Silent Footsteps

Trixie Duvane thought she had it all: a loving husband, Lavell, and their cherished daughter, Miley. But the shadow of Lavell's past looms large.

Years ago, his fiancée, Hedy Malone, vanished on their wedding day, leaving behind unanswered questions. As Trixie navigates the seemingly perfect life in humid California, eerie footsteps echo in the night, hinting at secrets long buried.

Who is chasing the Nelson family? And what truth lies hidden in Hedy's abrupt departure? Dive into "Poise: Silent Footsteps" and unravel a tale of love, betrayal, and the haunting echoes of the past.

Unhatched Childbed

Jomi Ducille thought he could control his desires. An affair seemed harmless—an escape from his mundane life. But when it leads to an unexpected pregnancy, time itself feels frozen.

As his world spirals into chaos, Jomi grapples with guilt, fear, and the haunting weight of his choices. Reality blurs, and his mind fractures under the pressure. Can he reclaim his life, or is he destined to remain trapped in this unending moment?

"Unhatched Childbed" is a gripping tale of infidelity, consequence, and the struggle for redemption. Dive into this psychological journey where every secret has a price.

The Élan Hour: A Chilling Suspense Thriller Set in Marseille's Most Exclusive Nightclub

Hidden behind the velvet ropes of The Élan Hour—Marseille's most exclusive nightclub—lies a sinister secret. Every Wednesday, during the club's infamous golden hour, a select few VIP guests vanish without a trace. No bodies. No witnesses. Only whispers of a dark ritual that fuels the nightclub's power, wealth, and glamour at a terrifying cost.

When investigative journalist Nell Raine starts digging into the disappearances, she uncovers a web of betrayal, occult sacrifices, and the vengeful dead who refuse to stay buried. As the clock ticks toward the next golden hour, Nell must survive the secrets of The Élan Hour—or become its next victim.

The Allentown Mill

In the heart of an abandoned mill, an eclectic group of seven individuals finds themselves trapped, cut off from the outside world by a raging storm. As tensions rise and secrets simmer, the atmosphere shifts from camaraderie to suspicion when a shocking crime shatters their fragile peace—one of their own is murdered.

Kash Corvin, the freelance journalist chasing a story; Sophia Korr, the lawyer looking for an opportunity; Jett Voss, the charismatic daredevil; Alice Draxler, the compassionate researcher; Callan Mortemeyer, the cynical outsider; Millie Galloway, the optimistic student interested in history; and Preston Zelinsky, the enigmatic intellectual—all must navigate the treacherous waters of trust, deception, and betrayal.

As panic sets in and paranoia mounts, each character confronts their own personal demons while trying to unearth the truth hidden beneath layers of anxiety. With the clock ticking and suspicions binding them ever tighter, they must discover not only the identity of the killer but also what binds them together as people.

In The Allentown Mill, the walls close in on both the protagonists and the reader, crafting an atmosphere thick with suspense and emotional turmoil. As alliances shift and motives are challenged, will they unravel the mystery before it claims another life? Or will their darkest secrets become the very instrument of their downfall?

Delve into a world where every character holds a piece of the puzzle and no one is above suspicion. Find out what it truly means to be trapped—not just in a building, but in one's own heart.

The Girl On The Bus

On a greyhound bus from Manhattan, New York to Laconia, New Hampshire, Braythe Milton finds solace in the company of a mysterious woman with secrets of her own, Amity Stevenson. Her captivating stories draw him in, breaking the monotony of his business trip. Their conversation flows, each sharing bits of their lives. But when she departs at her stop, Braythe is intrigued and curious, left with more questions than answers.

A chilling twist awaits him, one that turns the seemingly ordinary journey into a nightmare.

As he continues his journey, Braythe discovers that Amity's departure is just the beginning of a shocking revelation. Who is Amity really? As the bus rolls on, Braythe's world turns upside down, leading him to question everything he thought he knew. An unforgettable trip awaits—one that could change his life forever.

With secrets lurking just beyond the window, Braythe must confront the darkness that follows. What really happened on that bus? Prepare for a ride that will leave you breathless.

A Clean Break, A Well-Deserved Disappearance (Beyond the Picket Fence: The Coastal Sisters Journey Series Book One)

Pushed to her limit by an oblivious husband and two entitled teenagers, a perpetually frazzled Tallahassee mom finally snaps.

She secretly plots the one thing she genuinely needs: a solo vacation, leaving her family to fend for themselves—or hilariously fail trying—in her absence.

LaToya Lawrence

The Sweet Scent of Tallahassee and the Stench of Tampa (Beyond the Picket Fence: The Coastal Sisters Journey Series Book Two)

In the heart of Florida's coastal charm, twenty-year-old Troy Buck awakens in a hospital bed with his mind a blank slate. His wealthy upbringing feels like a distant memory, overshadowed by one haunting question: what happened to him?

As clues surface suggesting he may have committed a crime, Troy is thrust into a whirlwind of doubt and desperation.

Alongside his wife Paloma, a criminology student, he must navigate a web of secrets and deception. Can Troy uncover the truth about his past before it unravels their future? The clock is ticking, and trust hangs by a thread.

Deep Waters, Dark Eyes (Beyond the Picket Fence: The Coastal Sisters Journey Series Book Three)

In "Deep Waters, Dark Eyes," the third installment of the Beyond the Picket Fence: The Coastal Sisters Journey series, join Ladonna Bradbury, Madeena Patton, and their diabolical niece and daughter, Paloma Moss, in an intertwining thriller and mystery.

The story involves an unsolved murder, a luxury cruise to the Caribbean Islands, and a deadly reveal in their own backyard at the quiet, exotic Lake Jackson cottage home inherited by the sisters from their late mother.

Lady
In this fictional California town of Ramona life is kind until a sudden flow of recent events come to threaten the immediate future of a young woman who is resistant to change and not prepared for the misfortune that occurs.

When all goes wrong, and Cora Eckhart's life turns upside down she chooses a path that leads into a world of uncertainty, instability, and risk.

Aware of the imperilment that she faces, Cora has a plan, one that eludes the law and those who are blazing on her trail.

With nothing else left but to fight and to survive, she takes on a double life that takes the lives of others in the survive of her fight.

As Cora unwittingly outsmarts others in her anomaly in crime will her luck eventually run out or will she escape into the new life that she aspires to create?

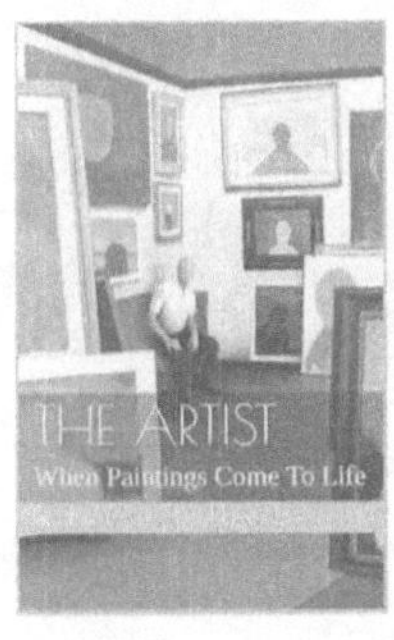

The Artist
Aspen is an artist with a hidden talent one that goes beyond his paintbrush and easel.

While he is successful in his work life as a cartoonist and comic book illustrator loved by both his sister Amiyah and his best friend Xander he suffers immensely in his personal life.

Aspen has no luck with the ladies. Women that he finds interest in have no interest in him.

They paint him out as one who they could not picture themselves with and there is no shortage to them expressing their unkindness and showing him their cruelness.

Fed up with the constant mistreat and disrespect from the objects of his affection, Aspen directs all his energy into the skill and beauty of his craft.

When his remarkably stunning works of art become recognized as extraordinary masterpieces women from the past have a sudden change of heart and now cannot help but find Aspen overwhelmingly irresistible.

As the ladies fall at Aspen's feet are they really looking at him through a new set of eyes or are they artfully led by the stroke of a brush?

In this cryptic tale of resentment and revenge—*a hand once dealt becomes the hand that deals out*—the man who the women could not picture themself with is the man who draws their life painting then brings their fatal portraits to life.

www.ingramcontent.com/pod-product-compliance
Lightning Source LLC
Chambersburg PA
CBHW020326180726
47991CB00019B/985